CARDCAPTORS
Sakura and the New Boy

Adapted by Kimberly Weinberger
Based on the television script by
Kathleen Giles and Meredith Woodward

THE CLOW

D1114633

SCHOLASTIC INC.
New York Toronto London Auckland Sydney
Mexico City New Delhi Hong Kong

ISBN 0-439-25186-9

™ Kodansha and © 2001 CLAMP/Kodansha/NEP21. All rights reserved. Published by Scholastic Inc. SCHOLASTIC, and associated logos are trademarks and/or registered trademarks of Scholastic Inc.

12 11 10 9 8 7 6 5 4 3 2   1 2 3 4 5 6/0

Printed in the U.S.A.
First Scholastic printing, January 2001

THE STORY OF
the Clow

Hi, I'm Sakura Avalon. I'm ten years old. And I'm magical! I didn't even know I had magic powers until I opened a strange old book. Inside the book was a stack of cards. They are called the Clow Cards!

A man with magic powers created the cards. His name was Clow Reed. He gave each of the 52 cards a different power. But when the cards were free to use their powers, they caused lots of problems. So Clow Reed sealed them inside a book — the same book I found!

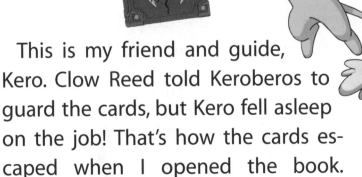

This is my friend and guide, Kero. Clow Reed told Keroberos to guard the cards, but Kero fell asleep on the job! That's how the cards escaped when I opened the book.

When the cards flew away, Kero lost his magic powers. Now we are working together to get the cards back.

Kero gave me a special key to help me capture the cards. I always wear it around my neck. When I say the magic words, the key changes into my Sealing Wand. I use my wand to capture the cards and return them to the book.

With the cards free, anything can happen. I have to capture them before their powers cause any harm. Wish me luck!

CHAPTER ONE
The Dream

"Oh, no! Not again!"

Sakura Avalon peered into the darkness. A large tower loomed before her. Beams of light danced in the sky.

Then she saw him.

"That kid!" Sakura gasped. "He has the Clow Cards!"

Suddenly, the boy leaped from a building and sailed through the air.

"Hey!" Sakura cried. "Come back! I have to —"

"Sakura!" called a voice from the distance.

"Hey!"

Sakura struggled to open her eyes. "Huh?" she mumbled.

"Snap out of it!" said the voice. "Sakura!"

"I can't! I can't!" Sakura shouted. She was still dreaming. She flung her arm forward, sending Kero tumbling across the bed.

"Oof!" Kero rubbed his furry head. "I hope you have a good explanation for that."

Sakura blinked her eyes. "Oh," she said. She tried hard not to giggle. "Sorry!"

"What's going on?" Kero asked.

Sakura explained. "I keep having that same dream. About this kid on a tower . . . with the Clow Cards."

Just then, a knock came at the door. Kero quickly put a blank expression on his face. He tried to make himself look like an ordinary stuffed animal.

Sakura's seventeen-year-old brother, Tori, peeked into her room. "Hmmm," he said slyly. He eyed his sister.

Sakura squirmed under Tori's gaze. "I'm up already!" she shouted.

"Sounds like you've got company, squirt, " Tori teased. "I heard voices."

Sakura laughed nervously. She glanced at Kero. "Everybody knows

stuffed toys can't talk, Tori," she said.

"Hmmm, "Tori murmured. "I think you are really losing it, squirt."

Sakura glared at her brother. "Get *out*!" she shouted. She hurled a pillow at him.

Tori closed the door just in time.

"Whew!" whispered Kero, stretching. "Why does he always do that?"

As if he had heard

Kero's words, Tori opened the door again. Kero stiffened and held his breath. He really tried to look like a stuffed animal.

"Oh, by the way," Tori drawled, "I'm leaving for school in ten minutes. So..." His eyes stayed on Kero as he slowly closed the door.

Sakura wondered again about her

dream. "What does it mean?" she asked.

Kero rolled his eyes. "Get over it, Sakura!" he said. "You have bigger fish to fry — like capturing the Clow Cards!"

Sakura knew Kero was right. Still, she could not stop thinking about that boy in her dream.

"Look, kid," said Kero. "You have to expect things when you least expect them!"

What's that supposed to mean? Sakura wondered. But she had no more time to think. She was going to be late for school!

CHAPTER TWO
The New Kid

"Tori! Wait u-u-u-p!" Sakura threw a quick "'Bye, Dad!" over her shoulder as she skated out of her front yard. Tori was already a block ahead of her on his bicycle. Naturally, her brother refused to slow down and wait for her.

"That's what happens when you sit in your room talking to yourself," Tori said when she finally caught up with him.

"I was not!" Sakura said hotly. She struggled to keep up with Tori on her in-line skates. She was about to say more when she suddenly caught sight of Julian, her brother's best friend. He was also on a bike, riding in front of Tori. In an instant, Tori was forgotten.

"The squirt was having a very deep conversation this morning," she heard Tori say.

Sakura blushed. Sometimes she wished she were an only child.

"Is he giving you a hard time again?" Julian asked her with a smile.

"As usual," Sakura answered. "See, I had this strange dream last night."

"Yeah?" said Julian. "Dreams can tell you what you least expect."

Sakura was surprised. The *unexpected*, she thought. *That's just what Kero said!*

"It's really quite amazing," Julian went on. "I had a dream this morning that I would have french toast for breakfast. And you know what? I did!"

Sakura giggled. She knew Julian was joking, but she still had a strange feeling. What unexpected thing would happen next?

Inside her classroom, Sakura sat with her best friend, Madison. Madison looked at Sakura through a small hand-held video camera. *"Another video camera?"* Sakura asked.

Madison's eyes sparkled as she swung her long, dark hair. "It's new. It's all digital. My mom got it!"

Sakura could not help but grin. Madison was always videotaping something. Usually she taped Sakura and her Clow Card adventures! Other than Kero, Madison was the only one of Sakura's friends who knew about Sakura and the cards.

"Good morning, class," Mr. Terada said. He was their teacher. "Take your seats, please. I have a surprise for you." He pointed toward the door. "We have a new exchange student. His name is Li Showron."

The new student appeared in the doorway.

Sakura gasped. *That's him!* she thought. *The boy from my dream!*

Li's eyes locked on Sakura's as he entered the room. He did not look friendly.

"That new kid is staring at you," Madison whispered to Sakura.

Sakura nodded. But she could not look away. She heard Mr. Terada tell Li to sit behind her. Still staring, Li made his way down the aisle. He stopped in front of Sakura's desk.

"Your seat is right over here, Li," Madison said helpfully.

Li slowly sat down. Sakura could feel him staring at the back of her head.

Oh, man, she thought. *Talk about intense! What does he want from me?*

CHAPTER THREE

The Fight

After school, Sakura headed outside to meet Madison. As she waited for her friend, Li Showron came toward her.

"Source of light," Li said, "with ancient spin . . . . "

"Huh?" said Sakura. "Excuse me?"

"Send forth the magic power within!" cried Li. "Oracles of Gold, Wood, Water, Fire, Earth, Clouds, Wind, Rain, and Electricity!"

Sakura backed away, her eyes wide with fear. She watched as Li held up a

strange spinning board with flash-ing lights.

"Force, know my plight!" he shouted. "Release the light!"

Blinding light shot forth from Li's board. Sakura stared in fright as it struck her. In an instant, the light returned to the board.

There was silence. Sakura looked up to see Li glowering at her.

"It *is* you!" he said menacingly. "You do have them!"

"I . . . have . . . what?" Sakura asked, her voice shaking.

Li was not happy. "This is a Lasin Board," he told Sakura. "It knows all! You have the Clow Cards!"

Sakura *was* scared. But no way would she let Li know! "Even if I do have the cards," she said, "I'm not

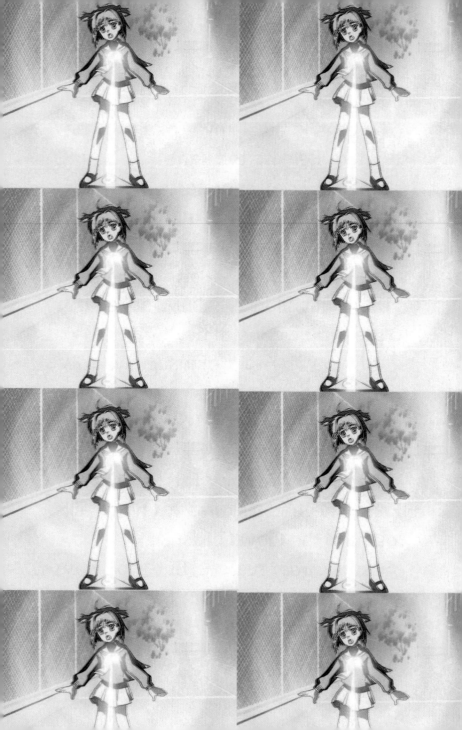

giving them to *you*! I'm capturing them for Kero."

Now Li seemed unsure of himself. "Wait a minute," he said. "Do you mean Keroberos? Since when does the Guardian Beast let someone like *you* handle the Clow Cards?"

Sakura told Li the truth. She had accidentally let all of the cards out of the Clow Book. Kero had helped her to capture some of them already. But there were still many more cards to find.

Suddenly, she asked, "How do *you* know about the Clow Cards, anyway?"

Li stiffened and glared at Sakura. "That's none of your business," he snarled. "But I'm taking over. Give them to me!"

Then Li *pushed* Sakura! She fell

back into the fence. She wasn't hurt. But she *was* angry. *Who does this kid think he is?* she wondered. Sakura fought back. Then she heard a familiar voice call her name.

"Sakura!" Madison cried as Sakura and Li struggled. "Hey! Stop it, Li!"

Li gave no sign that he was about to give up. But then, Sakura got some help.

"Hey, you!"

It was Tori, staring down angrily at Li.

"Don't pick on my sister, kid," he said. "Why don't you go home, before someone gets hurt — namely you."

Tori and Li stared at one another. Madison ran to Sakura's side. "Are you okay?" she asked.

Sakura realized she was shaking, but she didn't want Li to see that he had upset her.

"It was nothing I couldn't handle myself," she said unsteadily.

As the tension between the two boys grew, Julian arrived on the scene. "Anybody here hungry?" he asked with a grin. "Look what I have!"

Sakura watched in wonder as Li's entire attitude changed. A second before, he had seemed ready to fight her big brother. Now, as he stared at Julian, Li seemed . . . well . . . scared.

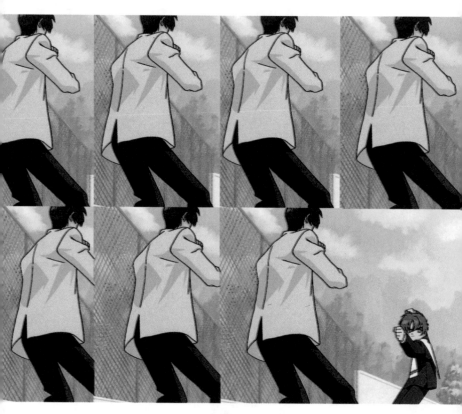

Julian didn't even realize what was happening. He happily held out a doughnut to Li. "Here," Julian said. "You want one?"

Li backed away and let out a strange cry. He turned and raced down the block, not looking back.

"Huh!" said Julian. "Guess he's not hungry."

After her fight with Li, Sakura was glad to take a calm walk home through the park with Madison. They were passing the playground when a loud crack of thunder made them both jump.

"Oh, great!" said Sakura. "A storm!"

Jagged bolts of lightning streaked

across the sky. The two girls ran for cover, then suddenly stopped in their tracks.

"That's weird," said Sakura, staring at the dry ground. "It didn't even rain."

The lightning continued to flash. Sakura wondered whether this day could get any stranger.

CHAPTER FOUR
The History Lesson

When she got home, Sakura raced up to her room to find Kero in a deep sleep. He was floating about a foot above the bed.

Kero grumbled when Sakura gently tried to wake him. Finally, Sakura drew a deep breath and shouted, "WAKE UP!"

"*Yaaooow!*" cried Kero.

Sakura was eager to tell Kero about her day. She tried to soothe her annoyed friend with a hot cup of tea. As she told her story, Kero calmly sipped the tea from a spoon.

"And he tried to take the Clow Cards!" Sakura finished dramatically.

Kero sipped his tea. "Expect the un-expected, Sakura," he said simply,

"That's it?" Sakura cried. "Kero! *He tried to take the Clow Cards!*"

Kero sighed heavily. "Maybe," he said, "it's time for a little history lesson."

Kero began to tell Sakura about his master, Clow Reed. "Magic is an ancient tradition," Kero said. "But my master created a new kind of magic when he created the Clow Cards."

Sakura was confused.

Kero tried to explain. "There are some people who study magic all of their lives. You could say they are born into the tradition." Then Kero said the most shocking thing of all. "Li Showron is a member of Clow Reed's family."

The news took Sakura's breath away. "If Li is related to Clow Reed," she gasped, "I should have given him these cards after all!"

"Uh-uh," said Kero. "It doesn't work like that. The cards were sealed in the book. You broke the seal. Only a person with special powers can do that."

Sakura looked doubtful.

"Don't you get it?" Kero said impatiently. "You are the one who found the book. You are destined to have the cards!"

The phone rang, but Sakura's mind was still spinning from all that Kero had told her. "Hello," she said. "Sakura speaking."

"Sakura!" It was Madison. "You have to look outside! At the sky!"

"Why?" Sakura asked, confused.

Madison giggled with excitement. "You have some cards to capture!"

Sakura opened her blinds. She peeked out at the dark sky. Flashes of lightning lit up the night. Thunder crashed over the neighborhood. Not a drop of rain was falling.

"Wow," Sakura whispered. "I guess I do. I'll meet you in ten minutes."

Kero cheered, "Now you're talkin'!"

Sakura wished she felt half as confident as he did.

CHAPTER FIVE

The Thunder Card

Sakura stared down at the costume Madison had made for her. Madison designed a special outfit to help Sakura battle each card. *Is this what a Cardcaptor is supposed to look like?* Sakura thought.

"Pink frills, Madison?" Sakura said uncertainly.

"It's not pink," Madison explained. "It's cyber-rose. It's high-tech, and it's in all the magazines."

"High-tech, huh?" Kero snorted.

"Nonconducting titanium and rubber," said Madison. "It will protect you from lightning!"

Kero had explained that the Thunder Card was causing the strange storm. Lightning was hitting buildings and trees. Sakura knew she had to stop the card before any people got hurt.

As lightning continued to fill the sky, Sakura got ready to take off. Kero had given her a magic key. Now, she held it and commanded, "Release!" The key quickly grew and changed until it reached its true form: Sakura's Sealing Wand. With the wand, she would be able to capture the Thunder Card and return it to the Clow Book.

Sakura held up the Fly Card she had already captured. Each time she caught a card, she was able to use its powers to help her capture new cards.

Sakura touched her wand to the Fly Card to set free its magic. The wand grew wings and quickly whisked her up into the air. Kero held on tightly as Sakura soared higher.

"Sakura," Kero asked, "did you notice if Li had some kind of magic device with him?"

Sakura remembered the strange spinning board. "Yes," she answered. "He called it a 'Lasin Board.'"

Kero seemed troubled. "That gives him an edge. The Lasin Board helps him find Clow Cards. It could be a problem for us." Seeing Sakura's anxious face, Kero quickly added, "Don't worry. You're the rightful Cardcaptor! We'll just capture that Thunder Card

before the Li kid shows up."

Sakura felt a rush of excitement. "That's right!" she said. "I'll show him!" But Sakura's confidence quickly turned to uncertainty as lightning flashes battered them from all sides. "Kero!" she called. "Just how am I supposed to do this?"

"First, " Kero said, "change Thunder to its visible form."

"And I do that *how*?" Sakura asked. But there was no time to wait for an answer. The lightning was getting too close.

"Jump Card!" Sakura cried. In an instant, she was able to leap from building to building. She finally landed on her school's clock tower. "All right, Kero," she panted. "What do we do now?"

But Kero didn't answer. Sakura heard an unwelcome voice say, "You really are pathetic."

Sakura and Kero turned to see Li Showron raise his sword. "Force, know my plight!" he shouted. "Release the light! Lightning!" In an instant, two bolts of lightning clashed and began to battle each other. Li expertly sailed down the side of the school wall. His green robes billowed behind him. *That's just like in my dream!* Sakura thought as she followed him.

Li's actions had changed the Thunder Card into a beast that looked like an enormous wolf. It roared and bared its razor-sharp teeth.

Sakura swallowed hard. "That's Thunder's visible form?" she asked.

"You are looking at Raiju, the thunder beast," Li sneered. "Boy, you *are* hopeless."

"Back off," Sakura replied. "The Windy Card will take care of this. Here!" She held the card out to Li.

"Put it away," said Li with contempt. "Windy can't stand up to Thunder."

Raiju's roars grew louder.

"You have the Shadow Card, don't you?" Li asked.

Sakura said she did. She watched as Li once again raised his sword. "Force, know my plight," he said. "Re-

lease the light!" Li pointed his sword at Raiju and cried, "Lightning!" Suddenly, Raiju began to rise up into the air. "Your turn!" Li called to Sakura.

"I can do this!" Sakura said. She touched her Sealing Wand to the Shadow Card. A ball of shadow formed around Raiju. She tried to remember the magic words she had used the last time she captured a card.

"Shadow!" she commanded. "Release and dispel! Thunder! Return to your power confined!"

In a brilliant flash of light and a final roar, the shadowy prison crumpled and disappeared. It took Raiju with it.

Sakura cheered as the Shadow Card and the Thunder Card floated to the ground. "I did it!" she cried.

Li walked toward Sakura. "Boy, you really don't have a clue about this, do you?" he said.

Sakura felt like a balloon that had just been popped. Maybe Li was right. Maybe she really didn't have a clue. She knew she would not have captured the card without Li's help.

"Hey, take it easy," Kero said to Li. "Everybody has to start somewhere!"

Li had not even noticed Kero before now. "What's this thing?" he asked Sakura.

"This is Kero," Sakura said.

"No way! K-Keroberos?" Li stammered. "The Guardian Beast of the Seal? The greatest Guardian Beast of all is a . . . stuffed animal?"

Hearing this insult, Kero angrily chomped on Li's finger. With a cry of pain, Li frantically shook his hand until Kero let go.

"Serves you right," said Sakura.

Li shot her an angry look. "You two are a joke!" he said.

Kero puffed out his tiny chest. "I was chosen to guard the cards by Clow Reed himself!" he declared.

"Hmph!" sniffed Li. "A lot of good that did." He turned and stalked away, nearly knocking Madison over as he left.

"Hi, Li!" said Madison.

Li grunted and pushed past her.

"Whatever," said Madison with a roll of her eyes. She saw Sakura and shouted, "Hey! My new video camera worked great! I got the whole battle on tape."

Sakura tried to smile at her friend but couldn't quite manage it.

"Hey," said Madison softly. "What's wrong? You pulled it off!"

"Yeah," Sakura said, sighing deeply. "But this is only the beginning."